THE PARABLE OF YOU

THE PARABLE OF YOU

STORIES

TONY WOLK

PROPELLER BOOKS
P.O. Box 1238
Portland, OR 97207

This book is a work of fiction. Names, characters, places, and incidents
either are products of the author's imagination or are used fictitiously.
Any resemblance to actual events or locales or persons, living or dead,
is entirely coincidental.

Copyright © 2013 Tony Wolk

All rights reserved. No part of this book may be used or reproduced in any
manner whatsoever without written permission from the publisher, except
in the case of brief quotations embodied in critical articles or reviews.
For further information, contact Propeller Books,
P.O. Box 1238, Portland, OR 97207-1238.

First U.S. Edition 2013

Cover and interior design by Context

Published by Propeller Books, Portland, Oregon.
ISBN 978-0-9827704-3-6

These stories previously appeared in the following publications:
"The Interview" in *Willamette Week*, August 8-14, 1985;
"The Minkfarm" in *The South Dakota Review*, Summer 1986;
"Borges: A Reading" in *Oregon English*, Spring 1989;
"The Nameless Ones" and "Two Black Swans"
in *Propeller*, Spring 2011.

www.propellerbooks.com

Printed in the United States of America

For Lindy

CONTENTS

The Nameless Ones • 11

The Shipwrecked Sailor • 15

War of the Invisible Worlds • 19

The Interview • 23

The Jogger • 29

The Woman Asleep • 33

The Woman of Scorn • 37

The Informer • 39

The Death of Danco • 43

The Stepmother • 57

Borges: A Reading • 61

Outside • 67

The Martian Invasion of the Invisible Woman • 71

Two Black Swans • 77

The Last of All Stories • 79

The Minkfarm • 83

The Parable of You • 89

THE NAMELESS ONES

There was once a beautiful young girl who lived in a land without lakes, far from the ocean. A zigzagging river ran right below the family cottage, its waters like ice from the glacier upstream. Water there was aplenty, for the river ran in all seasons of the year, even when it had not rained for forty days and forty nights.

Early in the mornings, whether it was dark or light, she would go down the path to the river with her two buckets and bring back the first of the day's water. With it she would scrub the wood of the floors as though she was a sailor aboard ship. After the floors came the table and chairs. Her mother who was not her mother would stand with folded arms and would point, and whether it was the spinning wheel or the shelf with its wooden owls, she would set it to rights, even when there was nothing amiss. For the spinning wheel was always in the same corner and the owls on the shelf did not have the gift of flight.

Rare was the word that was spoken to the girl.

Of course the girl had a name, which had been given to her by her mother and her father. But the woman who was not her mother, when she came to live with the girl's father as his wife, did not call the girl by her true name. Had her name been Susanna she would have called her *Annie*. If Mary then *Molly*, if Juliet, then *Rose*. When the father who was not her father came to live with the mother who was not her mother, her true name was altogether forgotten. Where you might expect to hear a name, as with *Anna, do this* or *Anna, do that*, instead you would hear *Wash this* or *Clean that*. Before long, without the benefit of words, the girl did what she was bidden to do.

Since I am neither the father who was not the father nor the mother who was not the mother, I will give the girl who was growing into womanhood a name: *Patience*. If I could, I would call her by her true name, her lost name.

Why, you wonder, would Patience be treated so harshly? I would give you an answer if I could, just as I would teach you the secret of the speech of birds if I could. If there lives a person who knows either the history of the woman who was not the mother or the father who was not the father, let that person come forward and speak the truth. Till then, I will say nothing more of those two nameless persons.

As I said at the beginning, the girl was beautiful. I will say that once more: Patience was beautiful, like a star that shines in the night with Purity and Constancy, which could be two more names for Patience. You ask, Did Patience know of her beauty? I can answer that question: No, she did not. The word *beauty*, as with many other words, had fallen by the wayside. Think of the word *beauty* as turned to dust. And without a word to anchor you, unless you are a beast of the earth or a bird of the air, you will see, but you will not see beauty.

One morning late in spring, Patience did not wake, not with the dawn, not as the sun rose above the snow-capped mountains to the east, not as the sun was disappearing into the valley below. The two nameless persons shook her by the shoulders as you would a rag rug. They brought icy water from the river, which they threw upon her face. They cried, "Wake up!" But Patience gave no sign of understanding. Yet they saw her steady breathing.

And so they sent for me. I will not tell you my name, for this is a story without names, and moreover, mine is of no consequence. What is of consequence is that I found a way to free Patience from the nameless ones.

The Shipwrecked Sailor

A shipwrecked sailor is washed ashore on an island which he guesses is either deserted or virginal to the foot of man. On the third day, after dining on wild fruit, he traces a stream inland and deep in the forest comes upon a small house. Small it truly was, with no more than its four walls and a roof. One of the walls has a small door, narrow and low, certainly not intended for his kind. Also, he notes, it's a door that slides open and shut. No visible latch, though within there might well be a way to secure it. A good kind of door on an island with wild animals, none of which he has seen, though in the night, as he sleeps in the crook of a leafy green tree, he hears their weird howling.

He is a cautious man. The weather is mild. The sea on which his ship was wrecked is not in frequented waters, though he has planted a flag fashioned from some jetsam washed ashore where he hopes against hope that it might be seen. For the moment he is safe, is well enough fed, and reminds himself that life back home was dull and constricting, which is the very reason he went to sea. The house shows none of the characteristic marks of abandonment: there are no mosses on the stones which are its foundation, no vegetation grows on the thatched roof, the stucco seems fresh enough. Even the sliding door, though he doesn't test it other than with his imagination, looks as though it would take but a fingertip to set it in motion.

Patiently, he decides to give the house its due. He waits one day, a second, and then on the third, when the sun is directly overhead, he is ready to put it to the test. By now the invisible creatures of the island are used to him. They see he bears no weapons, has no hostile intent, in a word, is harmless. Further, he would be strange meat—never before have they seen his kind. He approaches the house with a casual step. At the door he knocks twice, and twice again. Nothing, which is what he expected. With a flick of his left hand he nudges the door open. Within it is not altogether dark. He stands sideways, and crouching low, he enters. Behind him the door slides shut with a click. A spring mechanism of some sort, he decides.

Standing erect, he looks about and is surprised by what he sees. He is not inside the house as he imagined it, with simple furnishings: a bed, a table, a chair, a few objects scattered on a counter: a cooking pot, a hammer, nails, chisel, whatever. Rather, he is within a room—granted its four walls—but these walls are not just a few paces apart and the roof is far above his outstretched hand. He sees a long table with many chairs. Shelves line each of the walls and on the shelves are wooden boxes of all sizes. Chests with drawers every so often. The floor is made of polished board. In one corner is a wide stairway leading up to a second storey, these stairs to the measure of his foot. Yet behind him is the little door which would constrict even a child. On the far wall is another door, this one hinged, and its breadth and height in excess of his. The light by which he sees all this is thanks to two large glazed skylights on either side of the central roofbeam. The stairs, he wonders, will they lead to a tower, a belfry? Which of course he would have noticed right off from outside. He has the vague sense that he is being observed. He pokes about randomly, looking up and around every now and then. One of the chests is for tools, more tools than he has names for. There's a cupboard for dishes, another for cups and mugs. Another low down reveals a wide array of pots and pans. One drawer contains nothing but knives, some small enough for dining, others for carving, whether flesh or fowl or perhaps wood he can't tell. A tall cupboard with a high shelf reveals an array of stringed instruments, though none are familiar to his eye. What song would they play? What wouldn't he find here, he almost says aloud, aside from human habitation? He shrugs. Might as well try the stairs.

What stairs? He turns, uncertain what he will see, or not see.

War of the Invisible Worlds

I recalled [H. G.] Wells' dictum that in a tale of the fantastic, if the story is to be acceptable to the mind of the reader, only one fantastic element should be allowed at a time. For example, though Wells wrote a book about the invasion of Earth by Martians, and another book about a single invisible man in England, he was far too wise to attempt a novel about an invasion of our planet by an army of invisible men.
—Jorge Luis Borges, Commentary on "The Aleph"

I am My Tran and I am writing from my quarters on Tycho Brahe on Luna. I think I am the last human survivor. Today I will begin to tell our story.

First, I must admit that I am no storyteller—I am much happier with the impersonality of numbers than the slippery essence of words. And I will write in English though it is not my native tongue. For if this testimony is ever so fortunate as to find a reader, that person will not know so much as a word of Vietnamese.

All right. I will try to tell the story without going in circles. I do know where they have come from, from Mars, the Red Planet. Beyond that we know so little. (*We*—old habits linger.) It all happened so swiftly, first the sighting of the flares on the Martian surface, then the landings on our planet a few months later, and the blight that surrounded each vessel, the futile attempts at communication, the mysterious plague that took the men, and then the faltering of our women.

I write in the vain hope that the expedition to Alpha Centauri will not have failed. (You see I am back at the beginning. I am sorry. It is the best I can do). And if the expedition has succeeded, that it will return or at least send voyagers home to probe the long silence. I estimate my supplies will last me no more than a decade.

Again, I am sorry. I am trying to be clear, to tell the story from beginning to end, but I am overwhelmed by sorrow. I will try again.

I have reread the above. I am not a clear writer—that is what is clear.

The ships, I'll continue with them. They landed in a thousand or more places. All I can say is they fit our picture of a flying saucer, about fifty meters in diameter and shaped like a classical discus. The few eye witnesses who lived long enough to report said they saw a ramp extend from the ship, a door click open, and then came an array of objects floating down the ramp—boxes, tubes, vehicles on treads. Most watched in stunned silence. The lucky ones took flight. Those who stayed were never heard from again.

Does it matter what I tell next, how the military tried to attack the ships to no avail, the swift death of men across the whole planet, and then the women, that for a time it appeared Antarctica would be spared? Wherever a ship landed became like a desert, worse than a desert, since a desert is but another kind of ecosystem. But the immediate vicinity of the ships was a desert in the sense of deserted. Perhaps they deliberately sterilized the land (and air)—or it could have been an accidental property of their chemical being. Or a combination.

A thousand may sound like a great number, but given that the surface of the earth is vast, they were really few and far between. Before long they—I think I'll just call them the Martians—began to journey. To judge from their vehicles, the steering levers, the proportions, even the seats, the conclusion was that they were like us. They even had windscreens at an appropriate height. And from the experiment (costly to the experimenters) of firing colored dust at them, we confirmed our hypothesis. They were identical to us in every way we could discern. With one exception, of course.

The one theory I heard that made any sense was that they exist in a visual field sensitive only at the ultraviolet frequencies. Perhaps we were invisible to them. Yet just as we intuited them, so they must know who we are.

And then they departed. As inexplicably as they arrived. The boxes and cars and people (for I think of them as people mostly like ourselves) and an odd assortment of artifacts heading up the ramps, and the saucers drifted, away, home to Mars. Did they leave any colonists? None that we knew of. Did they take any of us? None that we knew of. We were too busy dying.

There is one thing I must not forget. It is not simply that their presence was our undoing. Again this is hypothesis. Strange as it may seem, they left behind thousands of their dead. And from the several autopsies performed, we ascertained the cause of death to be the most ordinary virus known to us. What merely gives us the sniffles, for the Martians was cataclysmic. Did they carry the deadly virus home? Was our presence as deadly to them as theirs to us? For it was a viral infection, and not any death ray, that wiped us out.

Is there a survivor, doomed like myself, on Phobos perhaps, who is telling a story to no one of the end of her race? Or has a Martian expedition already met ours in Alpha Centauri. I hope not, for their sake and for ours. Did they come in peace or in arrogance? Questions. I am My Tran, a peaceful woman of Luna, and wish you, the reader, well.

The Interview

My Uncle Sammy lives in The Amsterdam, a square, yellow-stone apartment house on Northumberland Street in Squirrel Hill, in Pittsburgh. He lived there with his mother, my mother's mother, from when I was an infant, and now he lives there alone.

He was everything to me as a child. We lived eye to eye, both of us watching my universe expand. Our vantage point was often my stamp collection—a stolid Mongolian soldier wearing a hat like a giant acorn, a sunrise in Azerbaijan, the Mauritanian desert, Tasman's Arch, frozen tundras in Tannu-Tuva. Sammy's pencil would trace the boundary of Mongolia and then sketch the anxious yurt from the inside looking out, a hint of dust on the morning horizon from the already approaching hordes of Genghis Khan further east. Time to be on our way. His stories rivaled Othello's haunting tales of anthropophagy and cannibals, of antres vast and deserts idle. What his stories lacked, his drawings supplied. And what he couldn't draw, he told.

It was Sammy who gave me *The Question Book for Young Folks*, which taught me such words as *hieroglyphics*, *cygnet*, *mutiny*, *Cossack*, and *semaphore*. And that the delicacy from the hoof of a calf is *calf's-foot jelly*, that the cunningest animal is the fox, that the oak tree does not shed its leaves in the fall, that air in natural motion is called wind. I'd quiz him, he'd quiz me. We were a perfect match. Where else could he market the fruits of his voracious reading? Who else could satisfy my boundless curiosity?

Meanwhile, my father came and went—his business left little time for me. Our lives barely touched. But I had my Uncle Sammy—until that summer of 1948 in Atlantic City. We four were staying in a suite at the Shelburne Hotel right on the boardwalk. It was early September—pageant time—and still warm. My mother and I swam in the ocean a little. But mostly we spent our time on the boardwalk, my grandmother usually in a wicker stroller directed by Sammy, my mother and I in tow.

Atlantic City had lots to offer, but for a 13-year-old, vacationing with his mother, uncle, and grandmother, with nary a friend in 300 miles—well, after two days I was high and dry, marooned. I discovered that the only one on vacation was my grandmother. The rest of us were her attendants. And the sudden intimacy with Sammy (I had seen less of him in recent years) was producing more friction than warmth. Literally, I took to dragging my heels. And then I made the mistake of complaining to my mother, "Why do we have to do everything she wants?" Sammy must have heard me, for a little later I heard him say to my grandmother, "He's just like his father."

Careless words in the heat of the moment, his and mine. But they were enough. In a flash I saw that he despised my father. And I made my choice and became my father's son.

Sammy's apartment has three rooms. Meals are eaten in the oblong kitchen at a drop-leaf table that is never opened. The bedroom that he and my grandmother shared for so many years is another small room with just enough space for the twin beds, a nightstand between them, a dresser and a highboy. Over the highboy are two photo portraits, one of my grandmother, the other of my young mother, taken at Kaufmann's Department Store, in sepia, 8 by 10.

The living room is lined with bookcases along every available bit of wall space. When Sammy was a child and his friends came over, instead of playing, they read. He never did stop reading. Now, when he runs out of shelf space, he packs up another box of books and takes it down to his locker in the basement, labeling it carefully, and then marking the spot on the map tacked to the wall— "Third shelf, South wall, Books, 7-24-49."

In 1976 he fell walking back from Rhea's Bakery on Murray Avenue and nearly died. It is two years after that fall now, and I am in Pittsburgh. One afternoon Mother tells me that Sammy has asked if I will come over.

He answers the door wearing typical Sammy clothes: a white shirt, frayed and unironed, and brown pants hitched up too high, the belt much too large now, its end looped around to the side. He lost weight after the fall. "Hi, kiddo," he says. "Take a seat." A few token words about visiting my mother and then into the interview.

His chair is just in front of a bookcase. Every chair is.

He reaches behind and takes a book from a shelf. The choice seems random. He passes me the book. "Do you know this one?" *Pig Iron* by Charles G. Norris. And in smaller print, "Author of *Salt, Brass, Bread*, etc." I open to the title page and then to the next. The dedication reads, "To Frank Norris." And then a short note addressed to "My dear Mouse," which reads, "Some 20 years ago your uncle dedicated a book to me—one of the things which, as you know, has given me the greatest pride and pleasure. So on this page I now place the name you share with him, in the hope you also will be glad to share the dedication." It's signed "Dad." I take a guess: "He must be the brother of Frank Norris, the American naturalist who wrote *The Octopus* around the turn of the century. He sounds socially aware, too."

I know I've passed Round One because Round Two is in my hands. *Sanine*, by Mikhail Petrovich Artsybashev. I nod. "Written just before the revolution. The despair of the young Russia dreaming of an impossible golden age, and Sanine the stalwart individual. I wonder if he's related to the man who did the covers for *Time*." Does Sammy remember my borrowing *Sanine* one summer when I was home from Northwestern? Good enough. Another pass.

The Brothers Ashkenazi by I.J. Singer. I see the sleek borzoi hound on the spine, a Borzoi book published by Alfred A. Knopf. "Isaac Bashevis's older brother. Another Russian-ish novel—a Jewish family living in Lvov, the center of the Polish textile industry in the late 19th century." I happened to have read it a few summers before when I was on a Singer kick.

Sammy relaxes. Like a tennis player at the net, he'd been poised, anticipating a next book if I had come up short.

It's a general pass. No more books to identify.

So Sammy tells me that because my life is stable (which means no divorces) and because I go on living in the same house, he plans to leave me his books. I don't have to keep them, but at least I'll know which is which as I discard or save them.

Oh, and I'll also get my grandmother's and his diaries, a continuous record of traveling in Squirrel Hill in the '20s, '30s, '40s, '50s, '60s, and now the '70s. Of going to Rhea's Bakery and to the Giant Eagle for cereal or the other odd grocery item. Never for very much. Only odds and ends, what with my mother bringing them our daily leftovers—meatloaf, brisket, peas, beans, cake. I never saw my grandmother cook in that narrow kitchen, not even to boil an egg, though I heard about her cooking from my mother as though it were legendary.

Will their diaries tell of hating my father? Will they tell of Sammy selling mothballs at a thousand percent markup all over metropolitan Pittsburgh, a sideline suggested to Sammy years before by my father? It was a suggestion that must have rankled, coming from the man who hadn't read a book in years, despite the privilege of the college education Sammy never had.

In a little while there'll probably be an entry describing Sammy's and my encounter, our interview.

What did my grandmother write? My mother would say her mother's diaries were filled with beautiful and inspiring sentiments. "Everyone loved Mother so." My guess is that they're filled with vitriol. Everything any of us at my father's house ever did that violated her three-room world. Anything that smacked of my father, anything that distracted my mother from absolute devotion to her mother. Anything that threatened Sammy's place in the universe. But I might be wrong. The saccharine could prevail. I wonder if Sammy will let me read the story of their bitterness? Does he have any choice?

I nod and say "sure" as he tells me his plan. What else can I do? *The Brothers Ashkenazi* is still in my hands, and Atlantic City is a long way away.

THE JOGGER

Abraham Lincoln sat on the stairs lacing up his shoes. Not even John Hay would join him on a day like this. Hay just shook his head when the Chief appeared at his door with running shoes in hand. And no use asking Lamon: his stately bulk required the clearest and mildest days for exercise. Strength he had in plenty, but durability on the road? Very little. It had occurred to Lincoln more than once that at the close of one of his speeches to the 19th Michigan or the 123rd New York State Volunteers, to add a footnote: *Would any bright young man, light of frame and with sound lungs, with the bitter experience of miles of marching through Georgia and Carolina, care to be a presidential companion in exercise? To wit, running to clear the pipes, refresh the sinews, and free the heart. Shoes and stockings supplied. Should have the ability to tolerate tales from Artemis Ward and Petroleum Nasby, as well as be resistant to tasteless stories from the Tycoon. An all-weather employer.*

Lincoln stood, stretched his back, twisted his hips, bent over and reached his fingertips a ways below his knees and above his tippy toes, took three deep breaths, then jounced his way to the entrance hall, opened the door, looked this way and that, and set off down the portico stairs, across the lawn, with a left at Pennsylvania Avenue past Seward's. Yap yap from Midge, Seward's notion of a watchdog. "Yap yourself," he called over his shoulder, though it weren't worth the effort. Still, you need to show the critter who's the dog and who's afeared.

On past Miss Arlene's Souza's, which past sundown doubles as a house of chance for the likes of Thaddeus Stevens and other casino haunters. It's the piano playing they go for—so they say. Pity all these music lovers couldn't put their heads together and persuade the armchair generals to find some other solution besides the execution of the death sentence for what they call desertion when a private does it, but term a strategic retreat when it's a high-tailing general like Rosecrans at Chickamauga. Seems every morning and half the days come midnight he was writing orders to *Suspend execution of death sentence for James Brown* or *Please make a commutation of this case as suggested within.* Left right left right post pone post pone.

Past the broken board with the rusty nail. As usual, after the first few minutes there is the temptation to fall back to a trot and then a walk. Then turn around before you become as sweaty as a baboon in July. Why push yourself on such a damp and dark day when there's a good chair by a warm fire? Which is why he preferred to have Hay by his side—you went twice as far in half the time, plus you got the bad jokes out of your system, to the great relief of Edwin Stanton. Better all around.

Huff and puff, huff and puff, clomp clomp clomp, his lungs taking in the fresh air—a good rhythm rolling—he felt like it could go on forever. Not that it could. For half an hour the euphoria would last, by which point the slope up to the Naval Observatory would take on a nasty character. He grunted at a passerby, a stranger with surprise in his eyes. Taking in the views of Washington City. Well, sooner or later he knew he'd be no better than scenery. Maybe after the war there could be a job with P. T. Barnum, in tandem with Tom Thumb and the Great Blondin.

Really, where would he go afterward? Home? He couldn't picture it. Life had taken on such a different cast. He'd just have to let time take its course. What he could picture, sharp as a razor, was himself that very first day in Springfield, back to springtime of 1837, and his breeches six inches above his ankles, a bundle of clothes on his shoulder and three dollars in his pocket. Himself the raw stranger and everyone else familiar with names and places and local habits. Come the third day he would gladly have given his last dollar to be back behind his Daddy's plow and assured of a home-cooked dinner. That was the day, the first day. The first time ever that he had traded Vulcan's boots for the moccasins of Mercury and took to the countryside. Cast aside his cares and woes and ran for his life.

THE WOMAN ASLEEP

Silvia Avogadro did not sleep alone that night. First there was her cat, Carulina, then there were the people who shared her dreams, who ranged from the Emperor Nero to a more recent but not too recent Italian who was dressed like an eighteenth-century dandy, both men playing violins. Nero she recognized thanks to his toga, his extended waistline, and of course his fiddle. What they played was exquisite, a haunting melody in a minor key, which summoned a landscape in Scotland, a loch, misty and deserted, with withered sedge along its shores. Partway through the dream she realized the second violinist was a quasi-namesake and ancestor, Amadeo Avogadro, at which point he removed his violin from his chin, set both violin and bow upon a nearby table, and began asking her questions about magic squares: "Do you know the 4-by-4? What about the four corners? Do they persist in each variation?" Each question she answered perfectly, which then led to the next, and ultimately to the last, pertaining to any even-numbered magic square, whereupon there was nothing more to know, the subject exhausted. He then kissed her upon the forehead, took up his violin, signaled to Nero. A moment later both were playing once again.

There was another dream shortly before dawn, very simple, that she was sleeping with a man who lay alongside her, facing the other way. She heard him wheezing slightly, which was what woke her. Carulina was sitting at the foot of the bed, watching him. Silvia knew this was impossible, that it must be a dream, except that she was wide awake. Lying there, wondering what to do, she remembered the earlier dream, but not the actual questions that constituted the examination from her revered ancestor. The dream, however, did suggest that if she could apply herself to the question, she would find a solution to the fundamental even-number magic square, discover its limits. And then it struck her, like a gentle slap across the cheek: to remember an earlier dream within the present dream was a sign that she was not dreaming.

Still, she couldn't bring herself to wake the midnight visitor, to tap him on the shoulder, to ask him how he had happened into her bed. Perhaps that wasn't the best question. She could begin, Excuse me, and once he was awake, she would figure out how to handle the moment. It would be an occasion calling for courtesy and diplomacy. For generosity. Yes, generosity. He would surely make his own excuses, ask her pardon, look around for his slippers and robe, and be gone. There was an alternative, of course. She could touch him gently. She noticed her knees were pressing lightly against his thighs. Since she was wearing her cotton nightgown, she couldn't tell if he wore pajamas or not. She pulled her nightgown up slightly and once more brought her knees closer and closer, till she knew it was bare skin and not pajamas. She was playing with fire. Who was this man? It was close to ten years since she had shared a bed with a man, with Leo—Leo who couldn't believe he was finally in bed with Silvia Avogadro. His disbelief was so patent that she didn't believe it either, and so requested that he please remove himself immediately. They had been at a summer conference in Locarno, engaged in the pursuit of mathematical wisdom. A request which sheepishly he honored, the fool.

She moved a little closer, the visitor's thighs accepting hers, as though they were accustomed to such intimacy. This had to be a dream. Was he wearing at least a T-shirt? No, his shoulders were bare. She placed her hand against his buttocks—yes, naked, completely naked.

She thought again of the man who came downriver, beached his skiff by a deserted village, and finally came to a house with a flight of stone stairs pitched against a side wall, ascending them carefully, for there was no railing and the light was sparse. And then the room with the book with nothing but her name written on every page. She wondered, Had there been a bed in that room? Was it also of stone? No, it would be an ordinary bed, like this, with a blanket spread upon it. The bed would be empty but she would know that someone had been sleeping upon it, for the blanket would bear the indentation of the sleeper. Had he given up waiting for her the moment before she arrived?

"Hello," she said gently, so as not to wake him. But it

was enough. He started at her voice, rolled over to face her, and screamed. Carulina rocketed off the bed. As in the story of the village of stone, she was alone, with no one by her side, no one.

THE WOMAN OF SCORN

"There's a story," Fedela began, "about a woman, a widow with seven starving children and just enough food for one. A man on horseback, though the horse was a *tsooli*, came by her hovel. 'Why are you weeping, my good woman?' The woman looked at him scornfully, this gentleman from the look of the gold tassels woven into his horse's mane and tail, as though his seat grants him the right to demand an explanation for what he's never before seen in his life, a woman grieving for her good-as-dead little ones. 'I'm weeping, good sir,' scorn again to the fore, 'that I have but enough to feed no more than one of my little ones for but a single day.' The man from high above surveyed the scene, the children ranging from infancy to no more than seven or eight years. 'And these are all your children?' 'You think some might be goats, or that I borrowed them? Have they not the print of my face?' 'You have good reason,' he said, 'to treat me with scorn, me with my fine steed, and my saddlebags bulging. I can do but little to ease your sad condition, but what little I can do, I will.' So saying, he rode on. When he and his fine horse were round the bend and out of sight and sound, she called after him but one word: 'Bastard.' She turned to her children, but not one was to be seen. Instead what she saw was not a wooden shack in sad disarray, but a fine house built of stone, neither too large nor too small, with glazed windows, a fine wooden door adorned with a carving of a flight of geese, their fine wings beating the air, and from the chimney a spiral of smoke. She looked again to the dusty road, but no sign of the stranger, not even prints from the hooves of his restless horse. Her gaze returned to the apparition, but it was quite real—a hand waved to her from one of the small windows, beneath which were an endless string of blue-flowered bushes such as her eyes had never imagined. She followed the flagstone path to the door, which opened before she could lift the latch, Tomas, smiling and dressed no more in rags. 'Madre, there's a cooked pig in the oven and an apple pie cooling on the sill.' She stared at him and the others now standing side by side at the kitchen door, their greasy fingers wiping their greasy noses. 'And you brats expect me to clean up this mess, and who will fetch water for the garden? I can read your squirrelly minds. Me, that's who. Now get out of my sight!'"

THE INFORMER

I'm trying to get my bicycle going at the Plaza Matteotti, the cobblestones thick with mud, worse than the aftermath of a flood, and as I pass under the old Roman arch, cars splashing mud left and right, a policeman hails me. "Antonio Rossi—that's you, right? A kid has just sworn that you've gone back to drink, so you better check in. Sorry, just routine, nothing to worry about."

I'm speechless. What kid? Little kid, big kid, split the difference, who knows these days? And why can't they clean up the streets, is that too much to ask? Too busy with informers. And while you're at it, get the *polizia* a decent uniform—tattered cuffs, mismatching stripes, boots left over from another century, another revolution. *Polizia!* There is no police, hasn't been since August, just what calls itself a Citizen's Army.

A voice at my sleeve. "Better get on that bicycle and out of here while the getting's good."

"Can't you see I'm trying?" I say, my foot doing its best to level out the pedal so I can swing aboard. And then behind the voice I see it's a familiar face, Giorgio, my brother's old friend back when the university was open to unreliables like me, his hair now streaked with gray. At his sleeve is a dark-haired woman in a long brown cape and high black boots.

"Topazio, this is Antonio, Guillermo's brother."

"Antonio," she says, "what are you doing alone here at the Arch?"

Before I can answer, she has me by my elbow and we're heading down to the river, the four of us, Topazio, Giorgio, me, and trusty Robin Hood, my left hand on the handlebars guiding it away from the throng at the Arch. We cross the Ponte di Zitelle and find our way to l'Ago di Cruna.

"What's this about your drinking?" Giorgio asks. We're sitting at a small round table, having ordered coffee and croissants.

"It's nothing," I say. "A glass of vino with dinner? You know it's nothing but an excuse for some worthless kid at the factory or l'Esercizio—who knows!—an imaginary slight, and suddenly they're filling out a form with my name with Drink as the reason. A hero!"

I nip off the tip of my croissant. Outside two old women in black are filling their plastic jugs at the fountain.

Topazio stubs out her cigarette and turns to Giorgio. "You believe his story?"

"No," says Giorgio. "You were right to keep your eye on him. Enrico is never wrong."

Buried in the folds of her cloak, I see Topazio has a shiny black barrel trained in my direction. "Don't worry," she says, "we'll take care of Robin Hood for you. And no rush. Enjoy your coffee."

THE DEATH OF DANCO

Survival (June 1, 1898)

The ice was quieter now, no hummocks in the immediate vicinity of the ship. The Commandant evidently relieved. For several days he had thought of little more than the imminent destruction of the *Belgica*, mesmerised by its constant shuddering, its groaning and shaking, its perpetual vibrations, the plaintive creaking of the woodwork—the ice maintaining its assault. At one moment he would remind himself and anyone within hearing of how magnificently the old ship was withstanding the constant pounding from the ice. Then he would fall silent, become as rigid as a statue, unable to deny the power of the pack, his poor little shell of a boat caught in the midst of such overwhelming forces. All the while, Roald Amundsen was overseeing the work on the two sloops, strengthening the keels, providing sails, their provisions, in the event the *Belgica* should be crushed.

In the midst of this crisis Danco lay on the stateroom sofa, gasping for breath. Breathing impossible on his narrow bunk "a passing indisposition" he termed it, his very words. At mealtimes he would join them at the small table, and come evening offer advice at whist. And the jokes, oh the futile jokes, to mask their distress. And the others, all so healthy, not even a single cold.

She couldn't bring herself to take up her pen. Soon it would be over. It was impossible to force-feed this gentle soul. She glanced his way. He was awake, his eyes shut tight, the chest rising, then rising further, till it caught a shallow breath. She got up, adjusted the cushions at his back. His eyes opened, his smile wan. She had never known such a stubborn man.

She returned to her station at the dinner table, opened her journal, and wrote.

> About six o'clock last night, with a stiff wind blowing, the ice about the Belgica fractured, and the ship slipped back into her customary berth in the water. We have survived, for now, the worst the Antarctic night has to offer. We have seen how strong our ship is. I wish I could say the same for Emile Danco. Strong-willed, that I can say.

She turned the pages back to the first days out of Rio, her first impressions, beginning with her portrait of the *Belgica*.

FIRST IMPRESSIONS. The Belgica is a three-masted ship, barque-rigged; 110 feet long, 26 feet wide, with a draft of 15 feet, with an auxiliary, steam-powered engine, set well aft so that her bow will rise to the ice & crush it. She is strongly built, with thick oak planks amidship, the bow & stern protected by 4-inch planks of greenhart, a tropical wood known for its hardness & elasticity. Quarters for the officers & scientific staff are aft, near the engine room. The men are crowded together forward, as is commonly the case.

The Belgica herself is pure Norwegian, built in Sandefjord at Christensen's shipyard, commissioned as the Patria, & put in service as a sealer. She is a stout ship, of about 250 tons, built about 10 years ago & in 1896 rechristened as the Belgica. The recommissioning, supervised by de Gerlache, produced a vessel that is slow & not particularly efficient (though no slower than the Archimedes which carried Father and myself to the Hecla & Fury Strait. Under sail, it employs roller-reefed sails, newly patented, intending that few men need be aloft in weather that is either bad or changeable, but like all things newfangled, they are subject to mechanical breakdown. The engine, I am told, is most efficient at 3 knots (it employs a type of internal-combustion engine, recently invented by Rudolf Diesel, perhaps the first such vessel ever to cross the Atlantic). Though its design is simple, the engine is badly placed & requires (in the words of Lecointe) a "thin boy" to clean out the boiler & reach its deeper parts. Its twin helms, or wheels, one at the stern for when the ship is under sail, the other on the bridge, are connected by a chain so long that neither wheel is supple as should be.

To stroll along the decks, the bridge, here south of Rio in the southern tropics, is pleasant, the crew already demonstrating familiarity with the vessel. For me, it is less easy, having surprised the Commandant & Captain & the others with the fact of who I am, a woman. What kind of woman remains to be decided, for the men of the Belgica, & for me as well.

The Commandant, Adrien de Gerlache, is a thorough man. He deliberately learned Norwegian, convinced of the importance of drawing on Norwegian experience in polar seas (Belgium with but 60 km of coastline, has a vastly different history of the sea from Norway). In July, 1896, Amundsen wrote de Gerlache, asking if there was still an opportunity to serve as a seaman aboard the Belgica. De Gerlache immediately accepted the offer, appointing Amundsen as second mate, a liaison in effect between the Belgian officers & the Norwegian men in the crew. The ship's cat is also Norwegian, its name Nansen.

On all my previous polar expeditions I was a known entity, daughter to Professor Richard Kiel, ever working in his shadow. Even when I had completed my medical studies & was serving in my professional capacity as physician to the expedition, I was still a secondary figure to my father. Now, for good or ill, I have stepped out of shadow & come into the light.

So the men go about their duties, sing, whistle,

grouse, climb aloft, scrub the decks, & pay little attention to the one woman among them. De Gerlache remains stiff with me. It was against his judgment that I was accepted for the expedition. Fortunately, the Belgian Counsel in Rio de Janiero spoke up for me, my having shed my horns while spending a week living at his house with his family. Captain Lecointe is a more genial figure, as is Emile Danco (the two men knowing each other from the artillery). Danco is a personal friend to de Gerlache. Roald Amundsen, the second mate, Norwegian & not Belgian, is a reserved young man, but entirely competent & well respected by all. The oldest person aboard ship is the Commandant, de Gerlache, age 32, just four years older than myself.

The men are half Norwegian, half Belgian. With the exception of Amundsen, the officers, & Henri Somers & Max Van Rysselberghe (the engineers), are all Belgian. The scientific staff is more widely European: from Russia, Poland, & Rumania (I will save writing a sketch of them, and Danco as well, for another entry.) I am of course from the New World, the only native English speaker aboard ship. Still it is a melange of tongues we speak, but is already sorting itself out: the men speaking a mixture of Norwegian & French when aloft; their own tongues when on deck & with compatriots. There is a subtle prejudice against the Norwegians, as though they are somewhat lazy & less earnest—not when it is Roald Amundsen's watch, naturally.

> Like Amundsen, a Norwegian, I am an outsider among the officers. Yet in my role as ship's doctor & for my polar experience I am vital to the expedition. Having brought a sledge of my own, my own clothing, my tent, skis, revolver & rifles, ammunition, tools & books & photographic equipment, I hope eventually to command respect. Grudging, I would guess. While we are still cruising in temperate waters, I am not put to the test.

An irony, the last sentence, thought Frida: a test which she could be construed as having failed, the rescue of Carl Wiencke.

She remembered how she had put off writing about the scientific staff, sensing a particular bias directed toward her as a woman with pretensions to possessing a scientific mind (with the exception of Emile Danco). Now, she depended on them vitally—especially Racovitza and Henryk. Like herself, they were not men of the sea, the *sine qua non* whereby the expedition would succeed or fail. Though that could readily change in later years—when the expedition would be remembered for its scientific discoveries. No, she thought, the world doesn't sing that tune. It is geographical adventure that commands the attention of the populace. And of donors, politicians, magistrates. Fridjof Nansen was a case in point: the confirmation of his theory of polar drift was less the story than his miraculous reappearance on the very day the *Fram* tied up in her berth in Tromsø. Survival in the face of tragedy, a better story than achievement thanks to thorough planning.

Danco, mercifully, had fallen asleep. And why had they

not allowed for polar anæmia? For that, she blamed herself.

Träumerei (June 5, 1898)

Daydreaming, she heard a melody from a piano, slow and dreamlike. Nansen at the foot of the bed, staring at her as though he too were hearing it. She hummed it aloud. Of course, "Träumerei," which she and later her mother used to play. The mother learned by mastering the piece a single measure at a time, the daughter by learning properly and sequentially. The daughter learned to play the piano; the mother learned to play individual pieces, three in all. Her mother began with no humble exercises, no "In a Bird Village" or "Twinkle Twinkle, Little Star" played one finger at a time. Instead she plunged directly into Robert Schumann—like going to war before you know there's such a thing as a trigger. "What if I were to play like that?" the daughter would ask. The mother would smile benevolently: "You have time on your side, my dear."

Her mother must have known what lay in wait for her just beyond the horizon. Mercifully, it was swift, the daughter just fifteen. Three pieces she played, never moving on to the fourth: Frederick Chopin, Sonata No. 7, Opus No. X; Johann Sebastian Bach, Prelude No. 1 from *The Well-Tempered Clavier*; and last of all Robert Schumann's "Träumerei." To hear her play, you would declare her a pianist. Who's to say she wasn't? Had she lived—but live she didn't, and the daughter treasured the memory of the mother's determined accomplishment, "Träumerei," most of all.

Enough loitering. Well past mid-day, and this would

be Danco's last day. For the last three weeks he had been unable to work, lying on the sofa in the wardroom, no other place affording comfort. The narrow bunks making breathing impossible. De Gerlache attibuting it to a defect of the heart. He had accepted his old friend Danco only after hearing that were he rejected, Danco would join an expedition to the Congo. *Perhaps*, Frida thought. Yet she couldn't forget Danco's stubborn refusal to eat fresh food—*Sooner die than eat penguin*. And the Commandant yielding, like a mother to a stubborn child—de Gerlache every bit as stubborn to her importunities on the necessity of a fresh diet. "Yes," said de Gerlache, "I know one emperor penguin would provide the dinner's centerpiece for the entire crew." Then his sour expression. "More plentiful than tasty." Knowing both seal and penguin fed exclusively on tiny crustaceans, krill. Better to dwell on the luxury of fresh-baked bread every day, theirs the foresight to bring along an abundance of sterilized flour. *Man does not live by bread alone*—she knew she was torturing the old adage, but its present application was too much to the point.

Frida rose, entered the wardroom. Danco lay awake and smiled upon her entry. He could not speak. Lecointe, who had been his classmate at military school, sat by his side, having been with him all night. Lecointe rose and yielded his place to Frida. Danco's arm lay palm up. Outside it was snowing once again. His pulse was feeble. It was too late now—all the months of canned foods, of *kydbolla* and *fiskabolla*, embalmed beef and fish. Oh, there were decent foods: breakfast cereals, hominy, coffee, marmalade, Michotte's fresh-baked bread. But endless tins of fruit and and fish and meats cannot sustain human flesh. Of course the answer to Danco's problem, to all their problems, was ubiquitous, would walk right up to them, fearless and foolish, a single penguin providing enough food to satisfy twenty-five men one day each. And good food, if you accepted the judgment of Roald Engelbreth Gravning Amundsen.

She found the Commandant standing at the wheel, though no open water was within sight. "Please don't tell me," said de Gerlache, his gaze steady to the west.

He was not a mean man, not at all malicious. Playing it safe would never get you beyond the environs of Antwerp. That he intended all along to winter over, that he falsified the observations, that he gave preference to his fellow Belgians, that and more she could forgive. But what about his bull-headed stubborness when it came to diet? She could label it blindness, could call him a creature of habit. Nor was the blame all his. What if Danco had thought less of himself and more of the others? What if he were willing to set an example? Why hadn't she taken that tack? He was such a generous man, and genial. Beloved by the crew. Yet absolute when it came to diet. She was sounding like Mark Antony speaking scathingly of Brutus. What, she wondered, distinguished the Belgians from the Norwegians? Inexperience with the Arctic? Proximity to the French?

"The germ lay within," said de Gerlache. "Don't we all experience shortness of breath one time or another? Did you anticipate this?"

"He would not let me examine him."

"He wasn't the only one. But I don't blame you. All that's in the past. And the men accept you, know your worth. So tell me, tell me the worst."

"He won't last another day. Lecointe is doing his best,

recalling old days in their regiment. But there's no response. He lays there inert. He did smile at me when he saw me, as though Death had come to welcome him to her house and he must be polite."

"What is there to do?"

"Nothing. Show him your affection, your love. He no longer has the will to breathe. He is waiting for you to appear at his side and then he can let go."

"I'll have Michotte serve dinner in my cabin, cramped as it is. And then we will go to him. Will that work?"

"Yes," she said. "I'll tell Michotte. The men have already eaten."

She informed Michotte. He nodded silently, a strong man and not shy of understanding. Outside again, she headed toward the bow where Amundsen was directing the work on the sloops. "Going well," he said. "The keels are ready, the sails coming along, masts and yards under way. You've spoken to the Commandant?"

"I have."

"What can he say?"

"Very little. So late in the day for words. And that I should be the one to inform him."

"You did what you could. We do ourselves a disservice when we place authority in one man's hands. Why would God give us a mind if we are bound to say, *Yes*? It's the condition of a man behind bars, without recourse."

"Yet you freely joined the expedition."

He looked at her askance. "My questions could've been more to the point, but I wanted very much to be taken on. You played the game one way, I another. Besides, you can never ask every pertinent question. Had I realized that he couldn't sail without a Norwegian officer— But forget all that. I am here by choice. We both are. Danco too, though this is day last for the poor soul."

"You think he foresaw this?"

"Yes. He's no fool. He understood the risk."

"Well, God be with him, but I wish I had been able to penetrate his armor."

"The man's a fatalist, Frida. Nothing you could say would change that."

She remained with Danco while the others had their dinner, and afterward they came in, one by one, and gathered round the sofa. Lecointe took his hand and began to speak of old days in the artillery, but gave up almost immediately, Danco's face emaciated and pale. Then his eyes opened, and his lips. "Thank you," he said. "I feel better."

His last words. His back stiffened, then eased—one final shallow exhalation and it was over. The passage from life to death, an invisible boundary. She closed his eyes. "Had he stayed at home," she said, "he might have lived another year, two at the most. Here he dies in glory, his name living on, a story we must live to tell."

"Yes," said de Gerlache. "He had been nowhere but Belgium, nowhere. Now we must tell the men—they will be heart-broken. The flag, Georges."

Together he and Lecointe spread the flag of Belgium upon the corpse, and so it ended.

Scurvy (June 6, 1898)

> As Roald says, "Now there are only six of us aft in the ship." The sailmaster prepares Danco's shroud, actually a canvas bag, the burial set for tomorrow. De Gerlache appears contrite. He has

sent the men an extra measure of grog. Upon my suggestion, the corpse of Emile Danco has been taken off ship and placed on a sledge beside the ship. The funeral is set for tomorrow. Just before Dufour took the last stitch, young Max Van Rysselberge placed in the folded arms of the now stiff body of his compatriot dried flowers, now faded, which his mother had given him at her farewell. An odd sight, here in a land where nothing flowers.

The appearance of contrition is insufficient. An act is necessary. The Commandant must live up to his title and command his men to change their diet. Yet until he changes his own tune, they will not change theirs.

I could kick myself for my kind-hearted words to de Gerlache, his grief impossible to ignore. I refer to my generous diagnosis that Danco would have lived no more than two years had he stayed at home, that now his name is an emblem for glory. I will no longer use the term "polar anæmia" but call a spade a spade, instead of the word none of us wish to hear, let it be "scurvy." Roald does eat seal and penguin, but as a Norwegian his example carries little weight—this is a Belgian expedition, after all, and everyone knows the odd tastes of the Scandinavians. My experience in the Arctic falls short for the very same reason: the diet of the Eskimo is uncivilized. Uncooked meat? As though it were not a matter of necessity when the only wood is the odd bit washed ashore by the accidental wave.

Funeral (June 7, 1898)

The men, having found no young ice anywhere near the ship suitable for the burial, had gone further and further afield. Eventually they found a recent lead and with chisels and axes dug the necessary hole large enough to accommodate Danco's shrouded body. The Belgian flag flew at half-mast from the mizzenmast. Shortly before noon, de Gerlache led the officers and scientific staff to the sledge. The men, clad outwardly in duck, then came to the sledge and took up the drag rope and drew the sledge southerly across the rough ice, the day 25 degrees below freezing and the wind out of the south-west with crystals of snow like needles piercing the skin. A misty day, with a faint metallic glow to the north, and overhead a few rosy stratus clouds. The moon, low on the southern sky and fiery, cast a weird light, bright enough to read by.

No one said a word as the sledge drew near their destination. Not since Carl Weincke, so early in the voyage, had there been a death, a time distant beyond measure, and sudden, unexpected. To assure its departure the men tied two sacks of coal to the feet of the shrouded body. De Gerlache with his gloved hands clasped at his chest spoke softly. "I do hereby commend to these southern seas our beloved comrade and friend, Emile Danco." No mention of the body finding any hospitable resting place. Not a word about glory or duty, no jingoistic girding of the loins for the challenge of the time to come.

The sledge then was tilted, and as the men were forcing the twin sacks of coal through the ice, Danco's body suddenly leaped from its place of rest as though alive, the canvas sheath disappearing from sight. The body bobbed once, twice, before its final descent. An upright burial, Danco not at all at rest beneath the ice, but set adrift. Before long drifting beneath the Belgica.

Officers and crew straggled back aboard ship. There had been no work for the men the day before and there would be none today. Danco's clothing was distributed among the crew, his other goods packed up and stored away.

Frida could think of no way to break the spell. So long as the Belgica was frozen in the pack, no seal or penguin could approach her. The barometer promised a shift in the weather. The ship took on an unpleasant list as the ice floes crossed one another. Nights would grow longer before they grew shorter; spirits would decline before they found hope. Roald climbed to the crow's nest to survey their situation and reported fewer hummocks to the south, but everywhere to the east and west. Not till spring could any movement be likely. Were there an orchestra aboard ship it would be playing a dirge.

She closed her journal and set her pen in the small jar along the ledge beside her bunk. When had she last seen a spiderweb?

THE STEPMOTHER

Mid-day, mid-April, 1865, and a break from chores, though chores of a Saturday were hardly worth considering. She was sitting by the fire in her rocker, her knitting in the basket alongside, Mrs. Stowe's book on the table at her elbow. Something about the day didn't feel right, though she couldn't put her finger on it. From the moment she woke, she was uneasy. She was sure it wasn't a dream.

Hopeless, an old woman chasing after dreams, who ever heard of such a thing? Dilly-dallying when she had yet to clean the ashes out from the stove. And there it was, plain as day. The trick is to give up the chase. She was taking a cherry pie over to Prudence Twilley and half-way along realized she'd forgot the sugar—nothing worse than a sour cherry pie. Could they sprinkle sugar on top to make up for the lack of sugar within? Like having your coffee with cream once the coffee is drunk. And she'd lost one of her shoes, not that she minded walking barefoot—it's easier to wash clean a foot than a shoe any day. So there she was hobbling along one-shoed with her sour cherry pie covered by a tea-towel and the next thing you know she's tripped on a root and is down on one knee, working her way back onto her feet, the tea-towel here, the pie over there—face-down. She brushed off her skirt best she could and picked up the pie tin, the pie no worse for wear—that's the magic of a dream for you. She took a pinch for a quick taste. Sweet as honey? How could that be? Now she has both shoes. Things are picking up. But which is the way to Prudence's? She's lost her bearings. Good thing it's a dream or she'd say she's lost her marbles. The road stretched out in either direction, each direction about as good as the other. Tears were running down her cheeks. Which is about when she woke up, the dream now as fresh as a daisy. And the tears still running. It wasn't the first time a dream had been forgot and then came back like a water buffalo.

She had been a widow for about dozen years. She didn't think about Thomas much these days, a hard-driving man, though a good enough man, considering. Witnessing the murder of his father—another Abraham—when he was but a boy, shot dead by an Indian. A terrible memory to carry forward. To his dying day that was the dream that would startle him awake, crying *What?* A severe man at home. There was no comfort for the loss of his daughter Sarah, the apple of his eye, to die that way, so neglectful. Spilt milk. And the day his son come of age. That was that, a kiss on the cheek for his stepmother and a close hug, and he was gone. Never did the father see the son again. It's the price you pay, the father hard-driving, the son at twelve with the strength of a grown man, his axe ringing in the woods, the two of them doing the work of three men. What the son said after the election and before going off to Washington City, how he loved her as true as any son can love his mother. The apple pie she had baked that morning was a real pie with real sugar and cinnamon and nutmeg and piping hot when they sat at table, with good coffee fresh from the grinder. He had seconds and then thirds. True, she loved him as one of her own, always had.

She remembered his sitting at her feet as she read aloud, *The Arabian Nights*, his favorite, unless it was that Crusoe book. Even back then he relished the idea of working for yourself, and no one saying git up you lazy lout. Thomas, if only you knew. The President of these United States, your own son.

CAST OF CHARACTERS, in order of appearance:
Sarah Bush Johnston Lincoln (1788-1869)
Prudence Twilley (alive 1865)
Thomas Lincoln (about 1776-1851)
Abraham Lincoln (1736-1806, killed by Indians in Kentucky)
Sarah Lincoln Grigsby (February 10, 1807-January 20, 1828, dies in childbirth)
Abraham Lincoln (February 12, 1809-Saturday, April 15, 1865, dies across the street from Ford's Theater, in house owned by William Petersen)

Borges: A Reading

Downstairs, Arcady Levin is about to write. He had gone up to the mountain with his wife Laia and her young son Mikhail for the holidays. They had hauled their supplies up from the main road by toboggan. Gradually the woodstove undid the chill, dinner was eaten, a few games played, and Mikhail was coerced upstairs, where he huddled under his blankets and finally fell asleep. After a little time alone, Arcady and Laia followed him up to bed.

About three hours later, Arcady dreamed that I was telling a story which ended with the words, "and he fires one shot." With that, he awoke. The story was no better and no worse than the stories I usually tell, but nevertheless, Arcady lay there alongside Laia, savoring its effect. He understood the story, though it took the very last line to convey its full meaning. All the pieces were in place, the pattern apparent after my deliberate evasions.

Arcady sensed perfection in the moment. The story,

its telling, his appreciation, the ambient snowfall. Laia nestled close by. And as an afterthought, Mikhail asleep. It hardly mattered when he realized that he couldn't remember more of the story than its last line. It was like the act of love with Laia—that the orgasmic moment passes and cannot be recaptured is no cause for regret. Still the analogy was incomplete. There would be other nights with Laia, but he would never hear my story again.

And so, Arcady is downstairs, crouching in front of the woodstove. Three good puffs and the fire blazes. He latches the cast-iron door and sits in the wicker chair alongside its warmth, pen in hand, notebook on his lap, ready to write. Not exactly the story he heard me tell, for that is forgotten, but a story which would present its reader with the same ideas as the story I had told.

Upstairs, Mikhail calls out in the night, "Mommy, Mommy."

"It's okay, dear, it's okay," says Laia, and Mikhail goes back to sleep.

Arcady breathes deeply, doubly aware now of the silent world which lies beyond his own breathing and the burning logs. He uncaps his pen and starts to write, beginning with the snow, the night, and the dream.

"Mommy, mommy," cries Mikhail. Then, gently, more to comfort himself with the magic of her name than to get her attention, "Mommy." Silence. But no matter. Mikhail is not alone. He reaches under his pillow, where he had left Defendor. He feels for the rim of the hatch, flips it open with his finger, and carefully climbs down the two metal rungs to the driver's seat.

On stage, Borges paused and reached to his left for the glass of water. He had moved a step away from the lectern, having begun the reading with the illusion of sightedness. He took a few sips, and then, before continuing, stepped forward boldly and conspiratorially.

"Don't let on to him," he said, gesturing over his left shoulder to the spot where he had been standing. "The story will be told without interruption. But inevitably I think to myself at this moment—though I have never written the thought into the story—that we writers are sly devils. It's our way of turning the tables on this stubborn, rigid, unaccommodating universe.

"It may be that your will is bound, but Mikhail's is free—I have created him so. And that bit of freedom shreds it all. So even the universe has its Achilles heel. Poof! Just telling you that he"—Borges gestured backwards again with a quick tilt of his head—"didn't pause and is telling you this story ratatat-tat is doing the Mikhail thing itself. Did he or didn't he? The old shell game. Enough digression. Recall, at last sight, young Mikhail had just taken the driver's seat." Borges resumed his reading.

Mikhail clamps the hatch down and is bathed in soft green light. He studies the interior of Defendor. It is in its compact six-wheeled tank phase. He loves the way it glows like a snake across the rugged ground. It is rolling steadily now over the barren terrain. Grandpa had sent the friendly GoBot tank for Christmas to help in the battle against the evil robots from GoBotron, to preserve life on Earth.

Mikhail's fingers move deftly across the glowing control panel. There is a faint crackle from the radio, and then a burst of alien garble. He picks out the word "Zod" and his back stiffens. He looks overhead at the yellow transformation lever, hoping he will never have to throw it while he is still inside. He wished he had worn his heavy field coat.

"Mommy," he calls once more into the night.

"It's okay, I'm right here, honey," she says, but she isn't really awake, and he is.

Ahead he can just make out the vague shape of boulders in his path. An enemy shot explodes nearby, and he sees the huge rocks clearly etched against the dull horizon and has no trouble steering around them. Still it takes every bit of his concentration, correcting his path with each orange flash. His temples are almost frozen against the icy metal of the vision port, but he needs the widest possible field of sight.

Up ahead, he can make out a hint of orange—Zod, the enemy robot rising monstrously on its rear wheels, about to transform. Mikhail sights carefully and depresses the firing stud. There is a red flash alongside Zod. A miss, but so close that Zod has to fight for his balance. Mikhail fires again, a little to the right. A direct hit.

He scans the battlefield warily—no enemy signs—and once again gives his complete attention to maneuvering in the silence of the night.

Borges paused and looked down and to his right, where Mikhail and Defendor were maneuvering. He smiled wryly, then took a deep breath and continued.

Downstairs, Arcady is busily writing. Mikhail doesn't bother calling for Mommy. He knows she'd just tell him he was okay. It's up to him. Squinting intently, he sees the orange light filtering up from downstairs. There is more of it now. It makes listening harder. He can hear better in the dark. Gradually the turbulence of his own blood subsides. Next he washed away the drifting of the falling snow on the slanted roof over his head. And then the gentle rise and fall of his mother's breast. Below now, worse than the rasp of a metal file, is Arkady's pen pursuing his hand across the page. Mikhail knows each letter, each word, each flourish, that the old fool is carving downstairs.

Mikhail adjusts the gun sight carefully, deliberately. There's no rush. He holds his breath. The two infrared images in the rangefinder flow together, and he fires one shot.

OUTSIDE

My name is Tony Wolk and I'm about one inch over six feet tall. Just now I nearly added on to that sentence, "and I've always been that tall." Trouble is, I was born. In 1935 my mother was five and a half feet tall, tall for her time, though she'd been that tall ever since she was sixteen years old back in 1920. Before 1920 she was shorter, and shorter, and shorter, and even shorter, until she was about one foot tall in 1904, the year she was born, my mother.

Of course she wasn't born my mother. Babies can't be mothers, can they? And I couldn't have been over six feet tall when I was born, unless I was born a giraffe. Imagine a giraffe named Tony Wolk.

Okay. My eyes are closed. I'm picturing a giraffe. It's outside, not inside, not in a zoo, for zoos mostly are made of insides made to look like outsides. Have you ever been to a zoo where you didn't have to go inside to see the animals? So, I'm right: zoos are all inside, mostly. And on the other side of the gate to the zoo is the outside. That's where I'm imagining Tony Wolk.

Tony is gamboling along with the herd, his brown and white legs ambling along, left, right, front, back. It's a wonderful feeling to gambol. I have an addiction to gamboling. So does Tony. And it isn't just because we share the same first name. It's a sunny day, and ahead is a grove of trees and beyond that the river. I've never drunk from a river, have you? It may come to that, you know. There's my father, and my uncle too, both craning their long necks to lap some cool water from the shallow river.

I'm still nursing. I've caught up to my mother—by the way, this story takes place in August of 1935, and I'm two months old. As I was saying, I like gamboling along, my legs stretching out like they couldn't, say, three months ago. I can still remember those long days, vague memories of unvoiced wishes as the time drew close, a dark time, a close time, wishing for what I didn't know what to wish for.

I've caught up to my mother. I'm standing by her side, catching my breath, listening to her warm breathing. She's looking back at me, my loving mother. I can read her mind, it's like time has come to a standstill, me and my mother, side by side in the gentle sun, the lapping of the river against the rocky shore, if only time didn't have to march on, inevitable, inexorable time, a war already begun, and then a wider war, a world war, and the whole world in flames, and death uncalled for. But now, right now, it's love, pure love, absolute adoration. My head is tilted upward, my lips are moist, and—oh, rapture—warm milk.

There's a picture of my mother, she's alongside my Aunt

Dorothy. They look so much alike, the two of them out for a stroll, beautiful beyond belief. I'm no longer two months old. I'm close to twelve. The world war is over, and the next war is biding its time. We're at peace. Briefly at peace. You can tell from the picture that whatever my mother is thinking about, it isn't me. If anything, she's aware that here, and now, in this brief shining moment, beyond the crabby reach of time's withered hand, that she's as free as the wind, strolling along the shore, with her best friend in the whole wide world, my Aunt Dorothy.

It's late. My mother lives on in pictures, pictures in my mind. I'm taller than my mother ever was. I wish I was shorter, just for a day, short enough that my mother was taller than me, short enough that my mother were alive and looking over her shoulder at me, so beautiful, as beautiful as the sun.

THE MARTIAN INVASION OF THE INVISIBLE WOMAN

I recalled [H. G.] Wells' dictum that in a tale of the fantastic, if the story is to be acceptable to the mind of the reader, only one fantastic element should be allowed at a time. For example, though Wells wrote a book about the invasion of Earth by Martians, and another book about a single invisible man in England, he was far too wise to attempt a novel about an invasion of our planet by an army of invisible men.
         —Jorge Luis Borges, *Commentary on "The Aleph"*

No one moved a muscle as the tripod touched down without even a wobble. The end of a journey that had been dreamed of for lord knows how long.

Collins looked at his two companions. Gleason sat, eyes closed as though in prayer. Hershkowitz was staring out the window as though a wicked stepmother had cast a spell on him for the next hundred years. Who could read their minds? And why was he wondering about them and not paying attention to his own thoughts? Maybe he was so overwrought that he had come round the bend into the ordinariness of what they had done. Isn't every morning an excursion into a new world? No sooner does the mind come awake and the eyes flip open but we are confronted with a time that has never happened in the entire history of the vast universe.

But just how chancy is the universe? What seems new to the unthinking eye may be no more than a warmed up yesterday. According to this theory, every day is provided for us by the heat of yesterday. The refrigerator is always full, but there are no stores for anything new. A moldy infinity. Is this flight to Mars a first, bright and shiny, or is it a journey whose inevitability became apparent in 1957 when Russia gave the West that catchy new word, *Sputnik*? Sooner or later technology and the dream of moving on would transcend politics. Common sense reminds us that it's not economically feasible to go to Mars, and especially foolish to send a person there when a probe can do all that and more. What else do you want besides a few sample cores, rocks, photos of the surface, measurements?

Well, it was up to him to break the spell. "Odd man out," he said, catching the pun as soon as he said the words. In his palm were three pennies. Now that they were under gravity once more, the flip of a coin became a possible moment.

"You're kidding," Gleason said. "Houston will kill us if Hugh doesn't take these first steps on another planet—politics says a civilian has to do it, like Armstrong. To show we're not a military venture. Ho ho." Of course all three knew about the mysterious package which would be left on Martian soil courtesy of General von Schirach.

"I mean it," Collins said. "And don't worry—the radio's still switched off. They're probably having a fit wondering what this extended silence means."

Hershkowitz was smiling. It meant more to him to play

a trick on NASA than to be the first human on Mars. The man's ego was as hollow as an egg shell. They were both looking toward Gleason.

"To tell the truth," she said, brushing the hair behind her ear, "I wouldn't mind taking a small step for humanity and a giant one for womankind. But if you're serious about the coins, it's still one chance in three."

"I am," said Collins, handing each of the others a penny. "One two three flip." He caught his coin in his palm and slapped it onto the back of his right hand. "Tails."

"Tails," said Hershkowitz.

"Heads," said Gleason, holding the coin out for inspection.

"Congratulations," said Rusty Hershkowitz. "Who would've thought the first Martian would turn out to be a female? And listen, let's just tell Houston I've got an upset stomach—you know how they don't want barf in a basket. And Ellen's the backup, anyway. Let's say we've reached that decision. Remember, we're on our own, and old Terra is only advisory. So suit up, honey bunch."

While Collins informed Houston of their successful landing and the slight change of plans, Ellen Gleason, with Rusty's help, donned her travel suit. No matter how much preparation they'd have on Earth, it was going to surprise viewers, laden with the reruns of all the Lunar walks, to see a person taking ordinary steps, at an ordinary pace, in unweighted boots. Add to that the evident breasts on Commander Gleason. "Ready," came Ellen's radio voice, and the next thing Collins knew the door of the airlock slid shut and she was gone.

"Strange," said Hershkowitz, "after all these months to have things happen in a few minutes. And nodding, he set the audio stud to open. "Commander Gleason has just commenced her egress."

The egress! Collins couldn't help but chuckle. This rehearsed line which always made him think of a new dance craze, performed stiff-legged in pairs. And what a pity there wasn't a camera already on-planet to catch the door of the spacecraft opening. Not till Ellen walked halfway round the spacecraft would she come into the visual field of the camera. And the windows were set up wrong—you'd expect someone to have thought of that, though none of them had. Ah, there was the thunk as the door slid open and the ladder unfolded.

"I'm now stepping onto Martian soil." Ellen's business-as-usual voice. "A small step for humanity and a giant one for womankind." Collins and Hershkowitz exchanged a thumbs-up. The boys in NASA were probably having a fit. Not that it wasn't exciting. There was no getting around the historicity of the moment. Collins' eyes were glued to the video screen for a sight of the first Martian.

"She ought to be there by now," said Hershkowitz. He was pointing at the Martian landscape revealed on the screen. "Ah, there she is."

And then, like a jovial butterfly of summer, Ellen Gleason, fluttering this way and that, was walking directly toward the camera, no doubt ready to flash that victorious smile that would be worth billions for the next Congressional appropriation.

"Ellen, Ellen!" Hershkowitz was screaming. "Are you all right!"

Collins looked from Hershkowitz back to the screen. Jesus Christ! Instead of a face inside her visor, there was nothing. Nothing. Just the bright orange insides of a space helmet.

"It's like a dream," the voice was saying. "Like a dream."

Two Black Swans

There were once two brothers, twins, each darker than the other, eyebrows, eyes, lips, and even their teeth. Looking at them, you would guess at the color of their bones, at the shadows deep in their hearts. Were they altogether alike? No two things are altogether alike.

One woman they came to love, her hair white as snow, her eyes as soft a gray as rain.

She loved them both, each for his own person. She loved the one who led the way and the one who followed. Time she spent with one and then the other. One, when she was with the other, would watch, like a dog with his eyes on a pair of swans by the river's edge. So came the day when one brother, the one who led or the one who followed, tasted blood, and his imagination took flight. He saw his brother with the woman. "It's time," he said softly as he drew his knife from its sheath. And so he slew his brother who lay panting by the side of the woman.

This story has its twin, where it is the other brother who does the slaying. And so in story there are two brothers living and two brothers dead.

THE LAST OF ALL STORIES

"Once upon a time—"

Hans paused, deep in thought, then began again.

"Once upon a time, not on the edge of a great forest but deep in the heart of the countryside there lived a man and a woman who feared one thing more than any other: light. The man had a long gray beard and when the woman walked she was hunched over. And she could barely see her hand before her face."

Here Hans' own shoulders seemed to shrink, his eyes to squint.

"When the woman was young she was tall as corn and could see the wagging tongues of birds from far away. The husband, he was sure of foot and his face was clear like the sky. And then came shadows into their lives. I won't say what those shadows were."

Hans paused, and now his gaze was directed downward, his body still.

"'Mother,' said the husband, 'I know what we must do,' and after his wife asked, 'What?' he answered: 'We must bury these shadows.' And so began the digging. They dug and they dug, and the deeper they dug, the darker were the shadows that followed the clang of pick and shovel. When they struck stone, they did not stop, for the shadows came on, darker than ever."

Hans sighed, his eyes closed, as though he was seeing the story unfold against his eyelids.

"Somehow they found food. Water they got from a small stream that trickled along as they dug. When they could no longer keep their eyes open, they would lie on a straw mattress, holding each other close. When they woke they returned to their digging. They did not know night from day. They heard nothing but the sound of their tools and their tired voices, hardly a whisper, 'Father, this,' and 'Mother, that.'"

Hans himself was faint of voice. "Is that the end?" asked Grethel when it seemed Hans would go no further.

Hans's chest rose and then fell, as though the story were borrowing his very breath with the telling.

Such a beautiful child, thought Alice as Hans gathered his wits. *And Grethel, too. What*, she wondered, *could have sundered this family, shed its mother?*

Before she got any further with her pondering, Hans opened his eyes and took a deep breath. He appeared dazed, looking at them or through them, as though they were phantoms.

"And that's the end of the story?" Grethel repeated.

A gesture of unknowing. "They're gone," Hans said. "Or they're going deeper and deeper. For a while I could still hear the clang of pick on stone, though it was no louder than the ticking of a clock. Is it stone all the way through to the center?"

"No," said the father. "The core is said to be molten, which means a hot liquid. No one could ever drill so deep."

Hans nodded. "I don't know where they were digging. It didn't look like this world. The sky was green and the clouds were blue. Is our sky ever green?"

"Never for long," said the father. "Such a sky presages a storm."

There were tears in Hans' eyes. "I'm sorry. I thought the story was going to be different."

The father nodded. "We can't always choose our stories or how they're going to go," he said. "Stories are a reflection of our lives. And the best stories are not reflections at all, but life itself."

The Minkfarm

Tonight the sky is clear, the half moon is waxing, and down the hall my son is soundly sleeping. In another room of another house, forty years ago, surely I slept just as soundly, and perhaps my father, another father's son, was then awake, as I am now, reliving his own childhood. Forty years from now, what will my son recall of his father beneath the waxing moon?

When my father was my two score and ten, he was a successful businessman and had been so for fifteen years, selling fur coats. Pittsburgh is a cold city in the wintertime, and in the 30's and 40's it was especially cold going to work. The women who rode on Pittsburgh's ill-heated trolley cars early in the morning sat on hard wicker seats and suffered indignities of the cold every time the doors opened. Buses were little better. That cold was my father's ally. Women came from miles around, from Oil City, Beaver Falls, Mars, Connoquenessing, Latrobe, and Johnstown, for the bargains that his sheep, rabbit, and muskrat coats most likely were, though the $75 coats they took home were called Mouton, Northern Seal, and Hudson Seal. A cheap fur, sheared and dyed, by any other name wears much sweeter.

My father also sold expensive furs, mink, broadtail (an unborn Persian lamb), leopard, as well as the middling expensive furs, black and grey Persian lamb, beaver. But the bread and butter of the fur business were those warm and inexpensive coats.

I knew little of this at the time. My contact with his furs was limited to occasional visits to his store, when I would slide open the glass doors of the display cases and edge between the velvety coats to stand quietly at the back. Customers would glide by, oblivious to the living being within.

At home I had my own fascination with furs. At night, in my double bed, I would be wedged against the wall by the row upon row of stuffed animals—rabbits, dogs, lambs, bears, and—foremost—the Panda family, presided over by a nameless female simply known as "the widow Panda."

My father and I spent little time together. And so it was a rare day when the ten year old child was riding with his father in their four-door, forest-green '41 Chrysler Saratoga. We'd driven east about fifty miles along the Pennsylvania Turnpike and then headed north into country more woods than farms. We spoke little. I was the custodian of the roadmap and of a slip of paper with directions that had been given to my father by Mr. Turner the day before. Sign followed upon sign, and eventually we spotted the mailbox with *Turner* written on it. We drove up the dirt road and behind the mink rancher's house, parking beside the barns. We got out and began our tour of the minkfarm.

I'm not sure why we even went there. I suspect it was more a whim than with any serious intent. The retailer and the rancher were at opposite ends of a chain. It was the New York manufacturers who bought the skins, and then not from the rancher, but at auctions in New York. Before the Second World War, almost all mink was trapped. Cheap mink was trapped in mild climates, fine mink in cold climates—the colder the winter, the richer the fur, the deeper the pile. Canadian mink were the best. By the 40's, trapped mink were called "wild mink," because by then there was enough domestic breeding going on, out of the wild. And the idea by then was not simply to increase the quantity, but to change the color, from the natural light or medium honey brown to dark brown. I suppose the darker brown looked thicker, more luxurious, maybe more like sable, the fur of the czars. The name of this dark brown was, strangely enough, not a color at all, but "ranch."

The Turner Minkfarm was set amid tall trees, with lots of shade for the rows of small wire cages set several feet above the ground. Mr. Turner led us along the rows. Here were the whites, here was a Kohinor—a piebald mink like a piano, a genetic sport along the way to other preferred shades. There had been a brief fashion for the Kohinor, but a spotted mink had its limitations.

"Careful now," advised Turner, a man about my father's age, but very different with his rural manner. "They may look pretty, but they'd snap your finger off if you give 'em half a chance. Watch this." He took a red handkerchief from his back pocket and stuck a corner inside a cage. Slash! "Okay? No touching, no petting." And so there was not much to do besides watch the sleek little dark brown animals pace back and forth in their cages, occasionally going for a bite of red meat or a drink of water at the front of the cage, sometimes going into the wooden shelter at the rear. What was there to do but follow my father following Mr. Turner?

I kept to the middle of the path. My father was dressed unusually I should say, though nothing like Mr. Turner in his corduroys and plaid shirt. I was used to my father in a business suit Monday through Saturday, in casual slacks and a golf shirt on Sundays, in his robe at bedtime. At home he always wore a white shirt and a tie. That day he was wearing slacks, one of his white shirts open at the neck, and a beige windbreaker over his green golf sweater. His shoes were his regular daily shoes. He asked questions about the breeding, where their stock came from, how long they'd been at it, when the kits were born, how long it took a mink to mature, how long before they could market the skins and still have enough for breeding. I hadn't seen any babies, not even any young ones. Except for the males being somewhat larger, they looked identical to my unpracticed eye. It was one to a cage.

My father's questions were partly polite, partly asked from interest. This was an aspect of his business, after all, and it would prove useful in selling to demonstrate expertise to Mrs. Rosebaum or Mrs. Anderson, Mrs. Cohen or Mrs. Levinson. "This coat is something unusual, very unusual. Ranch mink have been around awhile, but the newest strains of the ultra dark browns are just now being released into the market, and only experimentally. Really there won't be enough for commercial production for at least five years. It was obvious the moment I saw the animals myself at the Turner farm in Midville that they were a wonder, not only darker, but richer—just feel this. That's right, just gently with the back of the hand. Of course, mink is the most durable of all furs, but—my, isn't it exquisite. Well, to make a long story short, I implored Ed Turner to let me have enough skins for just a couple of coats, to show in the store, not even really to sell. Finally he gave in, and I had Mike Gainsborough make up just these two. There's nothing like them. Who even knows what they're worth? They're one of a kind. But how can I say no to you, Stella, after seeing what this gem looks like on you?" Usually the Stellas succumbed.

My father and Mr. Turner had stopped before the last cages in the last row, housing especially dark mink. They seemed even busier than the others. It was hard to imagine them at rest, let alone transformed into garments with monograms and silk linings, calmly walking about in downtown Pittsburgh. It was mid-afternoon and the sun was still sufficiently overhead that the farm seemed well-lit. We had seen what we had come to see. The thank yous and goodbyes that we were verging on were then interrupted by a strange procession. One of Mr. Turner's farmhands, a young man with sandy-colored hair, was leading an unsaddled dark brown horse by a rope to an open square filled with sawdust. Wooden posts stood at each corner, and one in the middle. Fixed to each post was a rope. The horse walked patiently, obediently, with none of the nervous pacing of its distant and smaller cousins caged nearby. The farmhand led the horse to the center of the square and tied it to the central post. Then, one by one, he tied the ropes from the corner posts high on each of the horse's legs. Making sure the knots were secure, the ropes taut, he stood back from the now tense and rigid animal. He backed away a bit further, picked up a rifle I had not noticed, stood facing the horse ten paces away, aimed between its eyes, and fired.

My father and I and Mr. Turner were standing off to

the side, watching. Only at the last moment did I realize what was about to happen. The shot broke the profound silence—my father had not said a word to me. I saw the horse shudder and go limp, its head slack. The four ropes kept it from falling. Then, with the shot still reverberating in the nearby trees, I realized that father's hand was on my shoulder, gripping me tightly, holding me close. I looked up at him—he was gazing off into the distance, his lips pursed as if he were holding his breath. And then—still facing forward—I was drawn within his embrace, his arms crossing around me, enfolding me, shielding me.

Fresh meat for the mink, Mr. Turner was explaining. My father, whose livelihood depended on animals dying to grace other hides, said nothing. I, understanding my father, assented to his silence. That night, at the dinner table, we described for the benefit of my mother and sister our day at the farm. Without prior agreement, there was no mention of the horse, nor did we refer to it afterward.

I would say that I forgot that day, that it disappeared from memory like so many other days. The sight of a horse or the presence of death is not enough to summon it from the recesses of memory. But unaccountably, at unexpected moments, like tonight, for I know not what reason, I have found myself standing rigidly by my father's side, the echo of the gunshot still ringing in our ears.

THE PARABLE OF YOU

There's a parable about infinity and its opposite. Physicists call it *The problem of the drunken sailors* and have a formula that goes with it, $\sqrt{d} = t$. The square root of the distance equals time. I picture it a bit differently, not with a host of dizzy sailors, but with one person who need not be drunk, need not be sober. You.

You are standing at a street corner. There is a lamp post by your side. You score it with a sharp stone, an X, or not just an X but a complex series of symbols. Perhaps you sign it. A child standing on a fireplug ties a blindfold around your eyes and spins you around. You step out, three steps forward, two to the left, four to the right, three back, an intricate and random series of moves north, south, east, west, and in between. Sometimes I picture an automaton, herky-jerky, left and right, back and forth. You do this for days. There is no sun, no moon, no life, no death. Just you blindly going this way and that.

A thousand years and you are still at it. The same khaki pants, the same wool socks, brown shoes, purple shirt, the same wallet with credit cards and driver's license and whatnot, and a $20 bill with lean-faced Andrew Jackson's wavy hair, his cape pulled tight around his shoulders. He doesn't age; neither do you. By now you may have crossed the equator. Always the landscape yields as you continue on your way. Except there is no way. You are not on any way, not on your way. Nor are you lost. What you are doing is intentional. Intentionally random. Randomly intentional. Voices come and go. The child who tied the knot on the scarf is years behind, is aging, has died. Her grandchildren have been born, made love, become parents, have died. The Douglas fir she loved along the Zigzag River has been spared the ax, is as tall as it can get, is nine hundred years old, is coming into its last years, crashes to the ground, is a nurse log for cedar, hemlock, fern, Oregon grape, trillium, Douglas fir. You are on the steppes of Asia obeying the ancient directions, steps left and right, back and forth, and in between, an ongoing combination that opens no lock. A Dante is born, condemned, and exiled. Her poem tells the story of her home and every other home, of never sleeping in her own bedroom or on her own bed. Midway in her life she has her vision, is led through Hell and beyond and finds the answer, finds her way home. You are in North Africa in a gentle rain, three steps forward, many steps to the right. Sometimes you count, sometimes you don't, and you come up against an object, rough to the touch, taller than you. Your hand traces the familiar scoring, the X, the series of grooves, your name. You remove the blindfold. You are on the corner once again. The universe is finite. In time, you will always come home. Always.

ACKNOWLEDGMENTS

For "The Death of Danco," Frederick A. Cook, *Through the First Antarctic Night: 1898-1899* (Doubleday, Page & Company, 1900, 1909; Polar Publishing Company, 1998); Adrien de Gerlache de Gomery, *Fifteen Months in the Antarctic* (trans. Maurice Rarity; The Erskine Press & Bluntisham Books, 1998); *Roald Amundsen's Belgica Diary; The First Scientific Expedition to the Antarctic* (ed. Hugo Decleir; trans. Erik Dupont & Christine Le Piez; Bluntisham Books, 1999).

Thanks to Dan DeWeese, who asked for more stories and over my objections and beyond my doubts received them, winnowed them, culled them, and perceived the story of stories, as Philip K. Dick would say, pattern-wise.

Thanks too to Molly Gloss, Loretta Stinson, and Shelley Reece for their enduring friendship.